Home In The Heartland

Renna Jo Damon

Copyright © 2020 Renna Jo Damon

Publication date: April 15, 2020

ISBN: 9798613223527
LCCN: 2020903902

Cover Illustration: Jim Guevara
Interior Format: Phyllis Clemmons
Editing: Phyllis Clemmons

FOREWORD

An automobile accident in Los Angeles, California leaves Marcia, age 17, Mark, age 5 and 3-year-old twins, Mandy and Melissa without parents to care for them.

The children have no other choice but to move to Ohio to live with their maternal grandparents, whom they have never met. These city children will need to adapt to farm living. The adjustments that need to be made, were a culture shock to them all.

Marcia meets and falls in love with a young man whom she discovers may share more than their love for one another. Her Aunt Ruthie tells her a story about her mother. A story that could mean the couple also share the same father. Marcia devises a scheme to find out the truth.

DEDICATIONS

This book is lovingly dedicated to my late husband, and biggest fan, Donald David Brown. Don gave me constructive criticism and encouragement to write.

I would also like to dedicate this book to my current husband, Douglas Paul Damon, who now offers the same kind of support and encouragement.

You have both been an inspiration in my life.

ACKNOWLEDGMENT

I would like to thank Mr. Chester Phillips, who was my creative writing instructor at Trinity Valley Community College in Athens, TX.

In 1988, after I'd stopped writing for a time, Mr. Phillips often told me that I had a gift for writing and he began to encourage me to get back to it. That was the turning point that motivated me to pick up my pen and begin writing again with renewed fervor. Thank you Mr. Phillips, for believing in me.

TABLE OF CONTENTS

TABLE OF CONTENTS (Cont.)

The Hope

It seemed as though they would never get there. They had been riding that smelly old bus for what seemed like forever. Actually, it had been only seventeen hours if you do not count the layovers in the far-out regions of civilization they had to endure to get this far.

Spending the day on a bus is no picnic. Especially with Marcia's younger brother Mark, and the three-year-old twins in tow. They were all on their way to live with their grandparents on a farm in Ohio.

Marcia was seventeen so she was in charge of the three younger siblings. Mark was five, but he was no real trouble as long as he had his big coloring book and his box of crayons. It was the twins that created the havoc. They were into everything except their seats. Anyone with a lap was fair game. Anyone with a snack was in danger.

No sooner had Marcia corralled one twin, then the other was halfway down the aisle toward the rear of the bus hollering, "Potty, Potty," to the top of her squeaky little voice. Nerves were on edge in that rolling, cramped, confined, chaotic coach. There was no escape, bringing a sense of helplessness to all the riders who, despite the fear of flying they might have had, were vowing to their seatmates to never take the bus again.

The children's parents were killed in a head-on truck auto accident only the week before. It was upsetting to them to be uprooted from their home and forced to travel such a long way to live with people they had never even met. They had not even seen a picture of the grandparents who would soon be raising them.

The children had never met their maternal grandparents because their mother, Margret had left home, never to return, when she became pregnant at the age of fifteen.

Maggie never married Marcia's father. Instead, she wed a man named Monte Malcolm

Murphy when she was 21 years old. They were married in a little cubby hole of a chapel in a small town in New Mexico when Marcia was only six.

It seemed Maggie and Monte started a tradition quite by accident of naming the children with names beginning with the letter 'M'. They liked to have never agreed on a name for the twins, though. Maggie named Marcia after the eldest daughter on a TV program she liked. When she and Monte had their first baby together, it seemed only right to continue using names that began with the letter 'M'.

So now the children were on their way to somewhere they had never been, to live with people they had never met. The kids had no idea what kind of reception they would receive. The couple had not seen their own daughter in over eighteen years.

Marcia was not thrilled with the prospect of living on a farm. For some unknown reason, she felt it might be good for the three little ones, but not for her. She was too tied to the city to live among the cow folk. Besides, she had a boyfriend in San Francisco she'd planned to marry if his parents would ever let him be free to live his own life.

Living on a farm held no impending intrigue for Marcia. She knew she would have to be allowed to drive herself, and eventually her siblings, back and forth to school.

Also, she would be looking for a job soon. She was not about to shirk her responsibilities by freeloading off of people she didn't know whether or not she would be able to trust. Displaced children are an easy target for evil. For her to trust anyone, even if she did share their last name, Marcia would have to adopt the wait and see option.

Although there would be insurance money forthcoming, it would not be enough to support three preschoolers until they reached adulthood, not by any means.

The call rang out over the speaker from the front of the bus. The driver announced his next stop. "Next stop, Chillicothe! Chillicothe, Ohio."

Marcia's heart sank as she realized this was the beginning of a brand new chapter in her young life. One that she would have to write about.

In the first six years of her life, she had been her mother's sole responsibility.

A sixteen-year-old on the streets of San Francisco with a child to look after was a horrendous task. Often, Marcia's mother had to trust strangers to care for her while she worked at some thankless job, making barely enough to buy milk and diapers.

A good-hearted couple, who had no children of their own, took them in. It broke their hearts to see a young girl struggling so hard to make a better life for her child.

Maggie and Marcia lived with them for about three years. They grew very close to the couple. Maggie even called them "Mom" and "Pop."

When she reached 21, she would be eligible for assistance if she had a place of her own. It was at that time, she decided to move on.
In the apartment across the hall from Maggie, lived a young man by the name of Monte Murphy.

"Mandy, Melissa, you two stay right here. I've got to go talk to the bus driver for a few minutes." Mark needed no instructions, he had fallen fast asleep.

As she approached the front of the bus, she said to the driver politely, "It isn't much further, is it? I'll need help with the children and our bags when we get there. Will there be someone there to lend a hand? There is a bus station here isn't there?"

The driver never looked up, but mechanical answered all of her questions in the order they'd been asked as if he had done so many times before.

She'd observed many stops and most only had a bench with a sign. Marcia had temporarily forgotten that her grandparents told her when they'd spoken on the phone to arrange for the trip, that there was a bus station at the Chillicothe stop.

She turned and headed back to her seat to gather her sisters and her brother, along with their meager belongings.

It was with mixed emotions that they left the dilapidated old bus. Stepping off that bus was the first step into the new life that awaited them.

"There they are," said Mark. "There's Grandma and Grandpa. I see them, I see them." He was looking at a couple in their sixties waiting near the baggage carts.

Mark had stereotyped what he thought grandparents should look like from his friend's grandparents. However, he was mistaken about this couple. They were not his grandparents. It became obvious when the lady who had been sitting across the aisle from them most of the trip, greeted the couple and left the station with her arm around the lady, while the gentleman carried her bags.

Mark, who was not yet ready to read, did not know that a lady was standing inside the door with a sign that read "Murphy Children."

Marcia saw the lady before she saw the sign. The woman was nothing at all like Marcia expected.

She was a tall, slender, redhead who wore an excessive amount of makeup for a farmer's wife, Marcia thought. This could not possibly be my grandmother, thought Marcia.

If this is her. We are going back to San Francisco! Marcia mumbled to herself.

"Hello, are you Marcia Howard?" The lady asked. Marcia nodded her head up and down.

"I'm Ruth Howard, your aunt. Your grandma sent me to pick you up."

Marcia was relieved to know the woman was not her grandmother, but she was apprehensive to learn how her Aunt Ruth fit into her family tree. Was this woman the exception or the rule regarding makeup and other aspects of her character?

The Homestead

Marcia put the kids in the car as her Aunt Ruth placed the bags in the trunk. Mark was put in the front passenger seat, as Marcia felt that was best. He kept his seat belt fastened and sat quietly during the drive to the homestead.

The twins, however; required more restraints. Marcia put them in the rear seat with some of the bags that would not fit in the trunk and she got in beside them. She had to refasten Mandy's seat belt twice even before the car pulled out of the parking lot.

Melissa started trying to open the bag in front of her, thinking her teddy bear was in it. Marcia tapped her little hand firmly and told her, "No"!

It was a short drive to the house, but it was a constant battle to keep the children under control. The excitement was almost too much for them. Melissa wet her pants for the first time since they started out on their journey. It was unusual for her to do that. Most often, it was Mandy who had such accidents.

Aunt Ruth turned up a dusty driveway that seemed to go nowhere. The winding road passed a forest of trees on either side and then back again to an expansion of wide-open spaces. In the distance, Marcia could see a large farmhouse, a barn, and a corral. There were all kinds of animals running loose in the yard. The only separation that kept them away from the house was a short fence that surrounded the house not far from the front porch. This little fence only kept the cows, goats, and horses off the porch. Ducks, chickens, geese, and smaller four-legged critters could come and go as they pleased.

The house was a two-story with a tin roof. It was white but in great need of painting. The house was surrounded by a wraparound porch. There were plants, chairs, benches, and bushel baskets on the porch. On the east side of the porch was a wringer washer. It was the kind that had to be cranked. There wear no electrical outlets visible outside.

Marcia wondered if there was any electricity inside the house. She began to wonder if they had taken a step back in time. *Just how rural was this place going to be,* she thought.

As Marcia stepped out of the car, she looked up at the huge window on the second floor. The room behind that window had to be at least half the size of the apartment they had just moved from. None of the windows on the second floor were dressed with curtains.

The upstairs appeared as though it had not been used in quite some time. The five upstairs rooms were fully furnished and decorated the same as they had been before Maggie left home. Since then, they had remained hauntingly unoccupied.

The grandparents moved down to the second-floor parlor when grandpa fell off the tractor and wrenched his ankle some fifteen years ago. They'd never bothered to move back upstairs again.

The entry was graced by the wide staircase that led to the upper portion of that grand old farmhouse. There was a clear sightline from the front door of the huge kitchen located at the back of the house. A fireplace in the kitchen crackled with a warm fire. There was a cast-iron stove, as well as a wall of free-standing cupboards lined up side by side and filled with home-canned foods and sparkling clean dishes. The pots and pans hung on the wall above the stove like some kind of artwork. The kitchen table was placed in front of the large picture window. Next to it was a very old looking quilt that appeared to have been hanging there for at least a hundred years.

The grandparents were waiting in the formal dining room (which had been transformed into a parlor and the old parlor is now being used as a master bedroom).

Grandma spoke first. "Did you kids have a good trip? There are cookies in the kitchen if you're hungry and your rooms are ready. I hope you'll like it here." She paused briefly before rambling on. "We are glad to have you. Just put your bags down right there. I'll help you get them upstairs later. Now, tell me about yourselves."

She spoke so fast, the kids were not able to get a word in or they would have rudely interrupted her. Grandpa just stood there, he knew better than to try to get a word in sideways. After a short moment of silence, Marcia felt it was safe to speak. She tried to answer all the questions in the order they were asked.

"It was a rough ride, but we did alright. We ate on the bus about three hours ago, thank you. I think we'll adjust well. Yes, I will. The bags are quite heavy. I am Marcia. This is Mark and these are the twins, Mandy and Melissa.

Marcia placed her hand on the head of each twin as she introduced them. Grandma could not comprehend how she was able to tell the two girls apart. They looked exactly alike to her.

The clothes were a little different but to the untrained eye, it was really guesswork in telling the two girls apart.

Anyone who was not accustomed to their differences would have to strip them down and check their navels. Mandy had a small but visible strawberry birthmark on the left side of her navel. Melissa had no birthmark at all.

After being around the girls for a while it became clearer, who is who and which is which. Mandy is the active one. She most often initiates the mischief. Melissa follows Mandy's lead. They do almost everything in tandem. Mark is the scapegoat. He seems to get dragged into the mischief while trying to redirect the girls to more appropriate behavior. What one does not think to do, the other does. They are very mischievous.

The girls get a lot of attention because of the mere fact, they are twins. This makes Mark feel unimportant, and therefore he remains quiet. The girls seem to get favorable attention even when their behavior does not warrant it. Marcia has learned to cope with this kind of situation.

Mark is good at entertaining himself. He would rather sit in a chair and color than chase a squirrel around the park and try to step on its tail, as the girls once did.

He hates to get dirty, (unlike the girls, who love to wallow around in the mud like pigs). He likes baths, (the girls fight every inch of the way to the tub). Mark likes all green vegetables, (the girls hate them). It is like trying to deal with opposite personalities in a constant struggle to be free at all times.

When a two-year-old suddenly faces the challenge of having a newborn baby in the house, sometimes he must sacrifice his quality time with his parents for the sake of the demands of the baby. But when the newborn turns out to be twins instead, sometimes he is forced to remain in the background too long. Problems lie dormant for years sometimes. Then all of a sudden something triggers the problematic behavior, much to the chagrin of the child's caregiver.

The Heritage

Grandma asked the kids if they were ready to go up and see their new rooms.

Holding on to the rail, the twins ascended the staircase to the second floor, where they would get to choose the bedroom that would be their sleeping quarters for the next ten years.

There were enough rooms for each to have his own, but the twins wanted to remain together in the same room. They made it clear they wanted to share the room across the hall from the room Mandy called, "Sissy's room."

Mark got the room closest to the stairs. Marcia's room had the big window that she'd noticed as they drove up only an hour or so ago. She wondered why it had no curtains. The bed was against the wall opposite the window. She would be getting plenty of good fresh country air with that window open. A dresser and chest were in the room that matched the bedstead. There was a picture of a young girl on the wall above the bed. The girl looked like Marcia! It was actually a picture of Maggie when she was about 10 years old. Marcia had unknowingly chosen her mother's old bedroom.

The twins had Aunt Ruthie's room and Mark had the grandparent's old room. The two other rooms had not previously been occupied, although one was furnished as a nursery. It would have been Marcia's room had Maggie not gone away.

The other room was empty. The walls were bare and the floor had no rugs. The window and shutters were closed and nailed to prevent anyone from opening them. daylight could be seen through cracks in the ceiling. The door to that room had been shut for almost as long as the Howard's had lived in that house. No one really claimed to know why.

Indoor plumbing was not installed in the house until 1926. At that time, a part of the porch was walled off and the fixtures put in. Access to the entrance of the bathroom was through the back door which was formerly used to enter and exit the kitchen from the porch.

Since it was no longer necessary to exit the house and trudge down the path to the outhouse, the door was not needed. However, Grandma missed watching her girls through that door as they did their morning chores each day. Once that entrance was closed off, she was no longer able to see them. Hence, Ruthie ended up doing more than her share of the work. Maggie was a little con artist. She would pretend to be doing something important and would ask her sister to do her work so she could do whatever she wanted to occupy her morning with.

There was no plumbing at all upstairs, so they made a water closet out of the second closet in the bedroom where Ruthie slept. This turned out to be very convenient for the twins. Marcia had no problem waiting until morning. Mark's room was located just a few feet from the bathroom at the foot of the stairs. The entryway was always well lit throughout the night, so he had sufficient light to take care of his business as often as the need would arise. The only problem seemed to be, the sixth riser of the staircase had a squeak that would wake the grandparents each time he descended the stairs.

The first night was restful. The beds were comfortable, the breeze was light and airy and the starlight was awesome.

There was the usual quiet supper with little conversation. The grandparents were used to the silence because before the children came, there was no one to talk to and the children were used to it because the walls were so thin at the apartment that every sound was like a shout that resulted in the neighbors pounding on the wall, as they often did in protest. Now, there was no noise.

At five o'clock in the morning, Marcia found out why there were no curtains on her window. No one could oversleep in that room. The sun shone through that great, big window like the beacon from an old lighthouse she'd once seen on a school field trip.

The sound of the livestock being awakened from their slumber could be heard from the window. The rooster began to crow just before sun up and could no longer be ignored. The combination of the loud cock-a-doodle-doo and the glare of the sunlight compelled Marcia to rise and shine. There was a wonderful smell that wafted up from the kitchen, of coffee brewing and bacon frying. Marcia dressed quickly and quietly went downstairs to avoid waking the younger children so early. To her surprise, the twins were already up. They were out on the porch in their nightgowns, throwing crumbled old cornbread to the chickens. They were laughing and having a good time. Mark was in the barn with Grandpa, being introduced to the farmer's end of a jersey cow.

Trying to teach a five-year-old how to milk a cow was a chore in itself. His hands were so small they barely fit around the cow's teat. Getting the boy to even touch the cow was not easy. He acted as though he was afraid he would make her mad or he'd get dirty, neither of which he desired to do.

What use is a farm boy who is afraid to get his hands dirty? *Maybe Grandpa should get the girls out there*, Marcia thought.

While Grandma finished preparing breakfast, Grandpa and Mark milked the cow, gathered the eggs, filled the water trough and pitched hay for the horse. The twins fed the chickens and other winged residents of the place and all of these chores were finished before seven that morning.

Although Marcia had to go register for school, she was not ready to do so just yet.

Being the new girl in school had its expectations. She did not expect to make many new friends on the first day. She was a senior and being a senior, transferring was usually not a good thing. Usually, the senior transfers were students expelled from another school. To keep them off the streets, they were allowed to attend a school elsewhere. Marcia did not want anyone to think she was there for any such reason.

She needed time to acclimate herself to the rigors of country life. She would rise at the crack of dawn to check out a few of the kids so that she could get a feel for how she would be able to fit in, wardrobe wise.

She had no idea how the school kids dressed in rural America. Most of her stuff was limited to jeans and shell tops. Although she had a few tube tops as well, she was not allowed to wear them to school. Marcia wanted to go shopping for school clothes before she actually started going to school.

She realized that if she put going to school on hold, she was also putting, making new friends on hold. There were no kids within miles of the farmhouse. All of the other farms in the area housed people from the third or fourth generation of the families who lived there. At one time, the children grew up and took over the farms. But now they grew up and moved away. Sometimes the kids didn't even wait to grow up, as it was in Maggie's case.

Leaving the little ones at home to be tended by Grandma was hard to do. Marcia had been their babysitter ever since they were born. Her mother worked all the time. This left Marcia the duties of cooking, cleaning and minding the kids whenever she was not in school. It took three incomes to support the family and now they were all gone. How were these old farm people going to provide the things a city girl needed to survive the materialistic world she had grown up in, and why should she expect them to? She did not feel right putting such a heavy burden on her grandparents. They did not owe her anything.

Nothing that happened between them and their daughter was in any way her fault. She never asked to be born. They were out of her mother's life before she ever entered this world, so why should they have any concern for her or the other children for that matter?

Grandma, on the other hand, was thrilled to have her grandchildren with her. She felt as though somehow, Maggie had come home.

Looking at Marcia, one would think Maggie had come home in some way. She was the spitting image of her mother. If someone thought the twins were hard to tell apart, they need only to look at the picture above the bed in Marcia's room to see two more who could have passed for twins if they'd only shared a birthday.

On Saturday, it seemed like the whole town had come to meet the Howard's grandkids. Grandma told everyone in town that the kids were coming. Up until a week ago, she didn't even know there were any kids.

What a life-changing event it was to suddenly find out you are a grandmother to three kids and a young lady.

Everyone appeared to be happy for the Howard's. It was not often that anyone around there got any of their family to return from the city. Once they left, it was nearly impossible to get them back, especially since no one seemed to value life on the family farms anymore.

Hard work and no money has little or no appeal to the younger generation. They want lots of money rolling in and landing in their laps while they sit back and relax in the recliner of their million-dollar suburban homes.

Marcia was used to hard work but none of it was ever outdoors. She was a good homemaker. She could cook, clean and sew with the best of them. She made most of the kid's clothes. With the exception of Mark's pants, she rarely had to purchase anything ready-made. Since the girls were out of diapers, Marcia had been making them outfits alike and keeping their hair clean and combed.

She made shirts for Mark from material that was not enough to make two of anything else. Often she got the bolt ends from the dry goods store, as Grandma would have called it. Marcia called it the variety store. Marcia loved to sew. She liked the feeling of creativity that she got upon completion of a project.

She was especially thrilled when the two outfits she made for the twins turned out well. Sometimes they looked better than the store-bought clothes the other kids wore. She liked the idea of saving her parent's money. This meant money not spent on clothes that would soon be outgrown, could be used for food that would assure the kids would indeed be growing. Nice clothes don't keep you healthy, good food does. Marcia made sacrifices for her siblings, not because she had to, but because she wanted to out of love for them. They kept her active, as it was a full-time job keeping them under control. However, she did it with a glad heart and a loving hand. She firmly patted their bottoms when they needed it. But also offered a tender caress when they were in need of comfort over a skinned knee or broken toy. She was like a third parent to her brother and baby sisters.

Now, is an opportune time for her to experience the life of just being a young adult with fewer responsibilities. Her first priority was to become her own woman. Her former duties as a co-parent to her siblings would be taken over by their grandparents. Marcia would now have the much-needed space to grow into the woman she was destined to become.

The crowd that had convened at the Howard farm included the Nance family. They had grown children who'd left the community like many others. However, they had a son they'd adopted, named Lance. The boy's birth mother did not want them to change his name. He was named after his father, as a bitter reminder that he was the grandchild and rightful heir to the richest man in town. No matter how he came to be, he was, who he was.

The Nance's honored the request to keep the boy's birthname so he was not Lance Nance. (God forbid anyone should have to go through life with a name that provokes laughter at the mere mention of it). The young man's real name was the bigger joke though. He was Lance Allen, III.

His father, Lance Allen, Jr. was the spoiled son of Lance Allen, Sr. who caused the farmers in the area to go belly up in the 80's.

He was not well-liked by anyone and his son was despised by everyone. However, his Grandson was loved by all. He had the best parents any kid could ask for. They loved him for who he was, not for where he'd come from. He was the product of the unwanted union between the butcher's daughter and Lance Allen, Jr. She hated him for what he did to her, but she loved her son. She arranged for the Nance's to adopt him even before he was born. He grew up to be a very well behaved likable young gentleman. That day, he met his future bride, Marcia!

The History

Marcia lay in her bed late that night, restless. Sleep eluded her as a stampede of various thoughts pounded through her mind. She was trying to remember the way things were before she left California. Her friend's face seemed to fade in her memory as she tried to visualize how her best friend, Joan had worn her hair. She all but forgot how they use to spend endless hours on the phone critiquing the other girls at school who were not as "cool" as they were. Clothes, hair, speech, mannerisms, reputations, family traits, traditions, skeletons, and class all serve to influence popularity. Nothing was beyond the boundaries of their scrutiny. No one was safe from being the "main course" primed, served and devoured by the ravenous fangs of their vicious conversations. They could pick a person apart better than a buzzard on road kill any day of the week.

Marcia decided she did not want that kind of friend any longer. She did not want to be that kind of person anymore. She wanted to see the good in people. She certainly saw plenty of it in Lance Allen.

A smile came across her face as she thought of him. He'd made quite an impression on her. She curled up in her bed and hugged herself tightly as the memories so recently engraved into her senses came back to tease her emotions. She remembered how nice he smelled and the soft-spoken manner he used to voice his words. He was also an attentive listener and was incredibly handsome.

Marcia thought she could not be in love with Lance. She did not believe in love at first sight, or did she? She just may have quite possibly fallen in love with the first young man she laid eyes on since coming to Ohio.

Marcia wondered if Lance was as impressed with her as she was with him. She envisioned the two of them at the Cotillion or the County Fair together. She imagined each scenario down to the smallest detail. Everything from what she wore to what they talked about and who else was there, crowded her mind until she drifted off to sleep only to continue the events in her dreams.

Marcia woke up in a joyful mood even though she did not fall asleep until after three o'clock in the morning. She sang softly to herself as her thoughts raced back to the delightful dream she had awakened from. As she was making her bed, she pretended it was her grandmother's big checkered tablecloth she was flinging into the air to place on the ground for her and Lance to lie upon while enjoying a picnic lunch at the pond.

Marcia was actually unaware that there was a pond on the farm. She had not explored the property past the barn since she arrived.

The Heartthrob

Lance woke that morning with Marcia on his mind. He had a problem with that though. He had to figure out a way to break up with Cindy before he could approach Marcia.

Lance had been pursuing Cindy Lang since seventh grade. She had gone with almost every boy in the school before agreeing to go steady with Lance. She was definitely not into serious relationships. She did not go with anyone for more than three weeks. She made sure she was going with someone at gift-giving times, like Christmas, Valentine's Day, and her birthday. She was never going with any guy on his birthday.

Cindy was a most devious user. She played everyone. Lance wondered why he ever wanted to be one of her tokens.

Why wait for a bus when you could have a Mercedes? Well, it felt like he had caught the bus just as the Mercedes pulled up to the curb.

How could he break it off with Cindy? Should he wait until she got ready to break up with him? That solution would spare him a lot of grief and misery.

When Lance arrived at school, he was greeted by the coach who was showing a new boy around the campus. Coach introduced the boy to him as Blake Daniels. He asked Lance if he would take over the tour for him as he had another appointment.

Blake was tall, slender and had a peach-fuzz mustache. He was eighteen and in the tenth grade. He was not a bad student, he just moved too often to have the opportunity to make good grades. He got left back a few times for low grades due to incomplete assignments.

Lance began to do something that was completely out of character for him, he began to promote Cindy to Blake. He told him all about her, leaving out the part about how fickle she was.

Lance told Blake how he had waited for three years to get a chance to go out with Cindy. This gave Blake the mistaken impression that Cindy was very popular.

Actually, Cindy had a false reputation of being easy, she was not. Perhaps this was one of the reasons she went from one beau to the next in such rapid succession. She would not allow herself to get so involved with a boy that she put herself in danger of compromising her virtue.

It was that very virtue that was being questioned. She was being labeled a tramp simply because she refused to become one.

Lance never doubted Cindy's values. He had known her since the first grade. They had at one time been next-door neighbors. Her family once owned the house next door to the Nance's until the elder Lance Allen stole it from them in a refinance scam. Her family lost everything.

Lance thought that if he could get Blake interested in Cindy and her in him, she would break up with him, leaving him free to court Marcia.

Lance had wasted his breath. No sooner had Cindy spied Blake, she was taken with him as if he were a movie star.

She did not even wait until lunchtime to corner Lance to give him back his ring. Lance had mixed emotions about the breakup, but in his heart, he knew she was not the girl for him, so he was somewhat relieved.

After he'd waited a while, one day just before the final bell rang, he asked Marcia to go out with him.

Marcia accepted the date almost before he could clear his throat. "Saturday, your house at two o'clock," he said. Then they both boarded their respective bus for the ride home. Marcia smiled as she heard a "Whoop, Whoop," coming from Lance's bus.

It was a beautiful day for a picnic. There was a gentle breeze blowing the wind upward from the Purina dog food plant, thankfully. (The air can smell quite unpleasant when the wind picks up the scent of the dog food cooking when it blows in any other direction, or the temperatures are hot and there is no wind at all). The trees were a source of welcome shade, and the sun was filtering through the boughs in a lovely light streaking manner, casting its shadows on the ground and on the pond.

The 37 ducks that considered the pond as their home, were noisy but pleasant. They had the good manners to keep their distance from Lance and Marcia's picnic spread.

The two young people propped themselves against trees where they could face the pond and still make that all-important eye contact. They talked about school, soccer, social events and relationships. They disclosed to each other most of their dreams and desires for the future. They also talked about their past and how it has made them who they are.

They mused over the fact that Lance owed his life to people who were not his biological parents, and how Marcia owed her future to folks who were not her parents.

Marcia compared her life to a tossed salad. Bits and pieces everywhere and no certainty about any given piece landing where it should be.

She felt lucky that she had landed all the pieces in a large enough bowl to keep her life as together as it was. At least she and her three siblings were not scattered to the winds. They have each other, and that is the best thing that has happened out of all the trauma the death of her parents had brought.

Time refused to stand still for the two young people. It was getting late and the sky was growing dark. Neither had a watch, so they did not realize they had been sitting under those trees for four hours. They packed up the remnants from the picnic lunch and headed for the house. Warm raindrops fell on them before they reached the front door. They stood on the porch just slightly damp and laughed.

No hug or kiss, only a friendly handshake passed between them as a salute to the evening of polite introductory conversation. Then Lance turned, headed toward his truck and drove away.

Marcia opened the screen door and entered the house. She placed the picnic basket on the kitchen table and ran directly to her room as a huge smile curled the corners of her lips.

In California, if a boy did not physically attack his girl at the door, the date was considered a failure. No second date was in the plans. This was not so, with Lance. He knew he had found the girl of his dreams.

Lance was embarrassed that his very existence was the result of Lance Allen, Jr.'s disrespect for a lady.

Lance loved the Nance's with all his heart, but he often wondered what kind of person he might have been if he had been raised by the Allen's.

The Holy Day

The twins had gotten into trouble with their grandmother the afternoon Marcia was on her date with Lance.

Grandma had bathed them and was washing their clothes on the porch in the wringer washer she's been using since her own daughters were small.

The girls had been instructed not to leave the porch, but they could play anywhere on it. As it wrapped around the house. However, the children managed to vanish from Grandma's sight for too long.

When she called them, they did not respond promptly. They had discovered the trough made of a fifty-five-gallon drum that had been cut in half and placed beneath the eaves of the house to catch rainwater. They had soaked each other by splashing the water. Afterward, they decided to help the chickens scratch for overlooked morsels of mash. This bit of action stirred up enough dust to lightly coat the flesh of the children to make them appear like Indian ghost dancers covered in ash.

A second bath was much needed and Grandma was the only one available to do the chore as Marcia had not yet returned from her picnic.

Grandma secretly wished she had a dollar for every minute her hands had been in water that day.

Sunday morning came and Grandpa was up early, as usual. He put on his new overalls and put a brand new bandana in his hip pocket. When he came in for breakfast, Grandma was shocked. She had not seen him this well dressed on a Sunday morning since their own daughters had left home over fifteen years ago. When he announced that they were all going to church, she was floored! He said, "If we are going to raise these kids, we may as well raise them right."

Mark had only been to church once and the twins had never been, so it was a novel experience for the three of them. Marcia used to go with her parents before Mark was born. It was more difficult to make the sacrifice with a tiny baby to care for and almost impossible when the twins came along, or so Marcia's mother, Maggie had reasoned.

The sermon was on the parable of the good Samaritan. This made Grandpa leave the church with a renewed sense of worth. He had been feeling like his life was not as productive in his later years as he expected it to be. All of a sudden, his life had a new worthwhile purpose.

No longer did he feel as if he had been trapped into late-life fatherhood as he did when the children first arrived. He was guilty of trying to convince his wife that they were too old to be any good for the kids. He wanted Ruthie to take them.

Ruthie was not a candidate for parenthood in any way, shape, or form. She was a flamboyant, eccentric, swinging, never before married, individual with nothing on her mind except where the next party was.

Grandpa thought, *if the children were in her charge, it would be the needed antidote it took to get her to act more responsibly.* Grandma did not want to use the children to force her to grow up. If she was happy in her lifestyle, why disrupt it if it would not be in the best interest of all concerned?

To Ruthie, the children were more like playmates. She visited often but never offered to do anything that resembled parenting. With the exception of buying them each an armload of toys, she did not offer her parents any assistance whatsoever.

She bought the toys for her nieces and nephew that appealed to her. They were toys she would have liked when she was a child.

Haven of Solitude

The twins got into Mark's new box of crayons and broke several of them. When he discovered the destruction of his crayons, he went ballistic! He told the girls he hated them and he wished they had never been born and that he was going to kill their teddy bears for what they had done.

This was the first time Mark had acted out since the death of his parents. His rage was excessive and inappropriate for the apparent situation. He had not progressed in the grieving process beyond any level of acceptance. He was bound to eventually explode. The crayons were just the trigger that released the rage that had lain dormant within him for the past few months.

He carried this anger further when he went up to his room to cry. While there, he decided he would just disappear. He went into the empty room and sat on the floor. Of course, he had his coloring books and crayons with him. He was in there for over an hour. Grandma called him but he did not respond.

Thinking Mark may have fallen asleep, Grandma went to the bottom of the stairs, called him again and waited. Mark still did not reply. She started up the stairs. Mark heard the squeak of the sixth riser and hid in the closet of the vacant room.

He thought to himself, *"If she loves me, she'll look for me until she finds me."*

Grandma went into Mark's room and did a visual search for the child, not seeing him there, she called him again. By this time, a bit of anger began to creep into her voice.

Mark thought he was in big trouble, so he kept quiet. Grandma went back downstairs without checking any of the other rooms. She returned to Mark's room moments later with a glass of milk and a piece of chocolate cake. She set the refreshments on the nightstand and left.

Mark heard the squeak of the sixth riser as she descended the stairs. Shortly thereafter, he came out of the closet and tiptoed back to his room. When he saw the cake and milk on his nightstand, he felt bad that he had acted in such a manner. He was not quite sure why he had done what he did, but he was now satisfied that his Grandma loved him.

Maggie and Monte had been married almost six years before Maggie became pregnant with Mark. They had almost given up on ever having children together. They were sure Marcia was destined to be an only child. Mark was a very welcomed surprise. He filled a void in their lives that Marcia could not fill. He was the product of their love. He was a Murphy, not a Howard. He was a boy and as such, he would carry on the Murphy lineage.

Mark got a rough start in life. He weighed only four pounds and six ounces at birth. He had to be put on a respirator for the first four days of his life. He had a low Apgar score (which is a method used to evaluate the condition of a newborn infant based on a rating of 0, 1, or 2 for each of the five characteristics of color, heart rate, response to stimulation of the sole of the foot, muscle tone, and respiration with 10 being a perfect score). Also, in the beginning, he was unable to suckle properly.

By the time he was able to go home, he had developed a very large appetite and was a wailing bundle of demands. This was a far cry from the personality he'd developed since the birth of the twins.

Marcia was already twelve years old when Mark arrived, so she was a tremendous help to her mom. She was able to feed, dress, bathe, and thoroughly enjoy her new baby brother.

Mark was only two when he was promoted to big brother. The twins were yet another surprise. Maggie did not know she was having twins until the prenatal sonogram confirmed it two hours before she was scheduled to deliver.

The doctors feared they would be conjoined as previous sonograms did not detect two heartbeats and only showed one fetal image. When it turned out that all was well and the girls were in perfect health, the thought of bearing twins was not so overwhelming. Add twins to a home where a two-year-old resides, is like having three newborns in the same household.

Mark reverted back to his pretoddler behavior. He became very clingy and needy. He was sure the babies had come to take his place. Sadly, in a way, they did.

The Handful

Using one's older children to co-parent the younger ones has long been a way of life in most cultures. Sometimes this practice is carried too far, confusing the smaller sibling to honor the authority of the caregiver over the parent.

This was the case for the twins. They would do almost anything Marcia told them to do. Nevertheless, if Maggie or Monte made a request, it was usually ignored until the parent became more assertive and raised his or her voice. Rather than get into a power struggle over minor issues, they delegated the duty of correcting the girls to Marcia.

As a result of the relationship the twins had with their parents, they didn't seem to miss them all that much. Unlike Mark, who was doted on for two and a half years, the twins were shared equally for the first two years of their life. Then when Maggie decided it was time to go back to work, Marcia virtually took over the care of all three children from two in the afternoon until bedtime.

Monte worked as a clerk in the auto parts department of a car dealership in Oakland, California. He also moonlighted as a taxi cab driver three nights a week. Maggie was a hairdresser by day and a private caregiver in the evenings.

Maggie's client was an elderly lady who was bedridden and required around-the-clock personal care. Her daughter lived with her but worked an eight-hour shift at the bank, two blocks from home. She was able to check in on her mother four or five times per day but when she went to pick up her son from school, she was not available to assist her mother for two hours. This is where Maggie came in.

It was not always an easy job. Sometimes the lady was quite demanding and other times, she was also verbally abusive.

The times Maggie had a hard day at the salon and a rough time with her elderly charge, she was not fit to care for her own children. This added hours to Marcia's day of co-parenting.

When Monte and Maggie died, it changed Marcia's responsibility for the children very little. The financial burden was the only thing she could not handle. That's why she wrote the letter to her grandparents.

Dear Grandma and Grandpa,

I know you don't know me, but I am your granddaughter, Marcia. You also have a grandson, Mark, who is five and twin granddaughters, Mandy and Melissa who are three. We need your help. We have no one else to turn to. We can only stay together as a family if we have a home where we can all be together and have some adults to care for us. I am seventeen years old and have been caring for the little ones most of my life. We have no money and we have no place to live.

Please call me at the number listed at the bottom of the page to let me know if you have room for us in your home and in your life. Thank you so much.

Your Granddaughter,
Marcia Howard

It was amazing, with no more information than that, Grandma called to tell these children who were literally strangers to them to come, The bonds of family are awesomely strong in a time of crisis.

Grandma lost her daughter years ago. Now she has lost her again, this time forever. But she gained four of the most precious young people she could have ever hoped to bring into her life as a septuagenarian.

Mixed emotions about having such young children to care for was swiftly swayed by the joy of having a new direction in life at such an advanced age.

Not many people get a chance to be a parent to a preschooler while in their seventies, (except maybe Abraham and Sarah from the Bible).

Grandma thought about her daughters and what she had done while raising them. She wondered what she could have done differently to change the way they turned out. Actually,

Maggie turned out great. It was the getting there that caused all the grief.

Everyone makes mistakes. Maggie's mistake, however, was colossal. She went to the haystack too early in her efforts to appear sophisticated. She wanted to know much more about a wicked world than she needed to know at her age. Her parents had tried to keep her safe, secure, content, and well cared for before she committed the deed that would put distance between them.

Maggie never told her parents who Marcia's father was. There were four possibilities. Maggie, herself was not entirely sure who fathered her baby girl, but Grandma knew one possible candidate was Lance Allen, Jr.!!!

Lance was an opportunist. When he was in his teens and twenties, he took advantage of every young lady he came in contact with. Lance Allen, Sr. paid for at least three abortions and paid to exonerate him from many other blunders he'd committed. Sewing his wild oats is what they called it. As long as he didn't hurt anyone, it was alright, but he did hurt someone! He'd raped Lance Allen III's mother!

The Heir

Lance III's mother was Becki Thornton. Becki's parents were the proprietors of the neighborhood butcher shop. It was one of the businesses associated with Lance Allen, Sr.'s enterprises. The Thornton's owed $55,000 to the bank Allen owned.

It seemed as though Lance Allen, Sr. had his hand in every pocket, in every pair of trousers in the entire town! This meant he pulled all the strings of business and finance, thereby controlling some aspects of everyone's financial position.

No one, except the preacher, could do anything without Lance Allen, Sr.'s blessing. He was not overly generous with his blessing, either.

When Becki became pregnant with Lance, Jr.'s child, she refused to be controlled by anyone. Not her parents, not the Allen's, not the community, or even her friends. She was determined to do what was best for her child.

Allen and his worthless son had the Thornton's so strapped for money, that they could not see any way they could possibly raise another baby. They already had eight children to raise and raising Becki's baby was just not financially possible at that time. It broke their hearts that they had to send her away, but it was for the best.

Allen thought she would probably put the baby up for adoption, but he did not expect her to give him to anyone locally. Nor did he anticipate Becki would insist the child carry the Allen surname.

Lance Allen, Sr. hated the fact that one day his son's bastard child would be the heir to his fortune. Jr. had managed to disavow all the other offspring, but he could not deny this one.

For one thing, Lance III looked exactly like his father. His eyes were set apart in the same way. He had the same dimple in the middle of his chin. They both had dense body hair, including arms, legs, chest, and facial hair which was an undeniable feature all the Allen men possessed.

Thanks be to God, he only resembled his father physically. Personality-wise, he was just like his adopted dad. He was humble, kind, courteous, loving, fair, and faithful.

None of these desirable traits could be ascribed to Lance Allen, Jr. or Lance Allen, Sr.

Mrs. Nance was the third-grade teacher at the country school where Mark would be attending next year. Mr. Nance was editor of the local newspaper.

They had three children while Mr. Nance was in the military. They moved around quite a bit in those days, so when the children had a chance to leave Ohio, they did.

Now the Nance's have a daughter in Alaska, a son in Texas and one in Georgia. The daughter is a doctor, the son in Texas is a stockbroker and the son in Georgia is an architect. There was not a black sheep among them. They were all doing well. However, the Nance's did miss being near their seven grandchildren.

Mrs. Nance mentioned to Mrs. Howard how much she envied her, having her grandkids with her.

When Mrs. Nance got a letter in the mail from her daughter telling her that she was expecting her third child, Mrs. Nance cried. That was another grandbaby she would never get to know. Alaska was just too far away to ever think she might go there for a visit someday.

Having the time to go was also a problem. She only had six weeks off during the summer to do any traveling. To go to Alaska without also going to Texas and Georgia seemed to be out of the question. Time was definitely not on her side, maybe when she retired.

The Honest Truth

Being the editor of the newspaper was a God-send for the Nance's as it was the source of information that led them to Becki Thornton eighteen years ago. If Mr. Nance had not been at the paper, he would never have known about the rape, as it was the catalyst that enabled them to get in touch with Becki with the hope they could adopt Lance III.

Mr. Nance remembered handling the story. He recalled suppressing the name of the victim to protect her wellbeing. His recollection of the mockery that ensued at the trial, and the way Becki's reputation was dragged through the mud at the hearing, made him wanted to spare Becki any more undue discomfort.

The judge ruled the incident was not rape and the line of paid character witnesses for the defendant was sufficient to dismiss the charge.

Once again, it was proven that money rules this world and answers all things. Every liar has his price. Wealth is a mighty sword. Wielded in the hands of the unscrupulous Mr. Allen, it was downright deadly.

All the time Becki was away, she was preparing to secure a good life for her son as well as make absolutely sure everyone knew who the child's father was. Judge or no judge, her son was Lance Allen, Jr.'s. She wanted to remind him what the Bible says is true. "…be sure your sin will find you out." (KJV)

Becki had been raped, but Maggie had given herself to Lance Allen, Jr., freely. She'd been sexually active with several young men. Fifteen is an unsettling age for a young girl. She was a woman/child at that age, playing with paper dolls one day, and lying in the hay with an adolescent boy with raging hormones, the next.

It was only by the grace of the Almighty that she did not get pregnant sooner.

Maggie had not been raised to regard herself in a disrespectful manner. She thought it was true that when a girl becomes a woman, she gets prettier. Those thoughts were due to the way her male companions wanted to have a roll in the hay behind closed doors but didn't feel she was pretty enough to be in their company openly.

Maggie never considered herself to be a Miss Universe contestant. On the contrary, she felt awkward, pale and skinny. Having a flat chest at fifteen was not a boost to her delicate ego, either. On top of that, she had Ruthie for a sister. Ruthie was Gorgeous!

She had curves in all the right places with an extraverted personality that made her socially accepted by all. She did not have to work at being popular, she just was. What was not to like? Ruthie was the kind of girl who would do almost anything for a friend, except compromise her values.

When Ruthie left home at the age of twenty, her values took a nose-dive. Although she steered clear of drugs, she found her freedom in bars, drinking and keeping company with undesirables.

Rebelling against their upbringing seems to be what young people do. At some point in their lives, most children disappoint their parents. Some try to reclaim their righteous selves, others never do come back to the family fold.

Maggie never came back to the fold. But she did settle down and make a good life for herself and her children. Marrying Monte was the best thing she ever did. He was good to her and he loved Marcia. He was her daddy as far as he was concerned.

Monte was an only child. He was the son of Hiram and Imogene Murphy. They migrated from Ireland in 1912. They had been passengers on the Carpathia, a British passenger ship whose claim to fame was that they rescued Hiram and Imogene along with many other survivors from the Titanic just before it sank.

The couple ran a dry goods store in the bay area for over forty years. This in itself, was noteworthy.

Hiram and Imogene died within six years of each other. He of Cancer and later, she of a stroke.

Monte, having no parents or siblings, meant there was only one option for Marcia and the kids. When their parents died they had to go to Ohio. Marcia was beginning to be glad they did.

The Hiding Place

Mark had discovered his hiding place. Whenever he wanted to be alone he went into the empty room. There, he pretended he was a lion in a cage or an astronaut floating in space. He could be anyone or anything he wanted to be in that room. It was such a sweet escape from being tormented by his little sisters.

One day, Grandma found the girls playing baby in the nursery. One was in the crib and the other was "changing" her. Grandma ran them out of that room, shut and locked the door. While she was at it, she thought she may as well lock the empty room door too.

Mark was in the empty room coloring in his big trains coloring book. He did not make a noise. He was so engrossed in his work, he did not hear Grandma lock the door.

When Mark did not appear at suppertime, Marcia became concerned. He'd never been late for supper since he was able to walk. It was unheard of for him to miss a meal. He was a walking digestive tract. He worked up an appetite just by getting up from the table. Once again, the search was on for Mark.

Since the window was nailed shut and the door was locked, Mark was trapped!

Marcia looked upstairs, Grandma looked downstairs. Grandpa checked the barn and the twins looked all around the outside of the house.

Just in that short timeframe, the draftiness of the room had caused Mark to develop Laryngitis, so he was unable to shout loud enough to be heard. The search continued and even expanded to include the pond and the road into town. Neighbors came to join in the frantic search for the boy who had fallen fast asleep in the empty room.

Night fell and still, there was no sign of the missing five-year-old.

In the morning hunger overtook the entrapped youngster and he began to pound on the door, the wall and stomp on the floor raising all kinds of racket.

Marcia was the first to respond to the noise. She unlocked the door and swung it open. There stood Mark, with tears running down his cheeks. She snatched him up and nearly hugged him out of his shoes.

When the boy tried to speak he could only manage a whisper. Hot tea and chicken soup soon had him back in fine voice. Grandma never locked that room door again.

Instead, she designated it as Mark's playroom. He alone was allowed to go into it.

As time went on, he began to invite his sisters in to play. Gradually he learned that alone, is not always desirable. Sometimes one needs the company of a friend.

By the time the twins started school, all of their indoor toys had relocated to that enchanted room.

The Horse

"Boy, get yourself out here," Grandpa called to Mark from the barn. "I got sum'n ta show ya."

Mark hurried to the barn to see Grandpa holding a very small saddle. "Ya wanna ride old Gert?" He said, with a gleam in his eye. "I don't know how." The boy answered. "Well, it's high time ya learned."

Ol' Gert was a twenty-year-old mare that Grandpa had gotten for his daughters to raise and enter in the county fair when they were 11 and 13 years old.

She was an orphaned colt. The girls had raised her, so she was like a part of the family. One day she marched through the backdoor straight into the kitchen and ate the corn Grandma had just washed for canning.

Gert was the reason for the little fence around the yard. House cats were okay. House dogs were okay too. But Grandma drew the line at house horses. She drew that line with her broom as she chased that confused little colt out of the house. Everyone laughed so hard, their sides hurt.

The only thing Grandma did while the fence was being put up, was to make lemonade. She saw no humor in having a half bushel of corn ruined and a horse in her kitchen. Those who found humor in that little stunt were put to work until they were sweating.

Mark's first riding lesson was simply getting to know Gert. He fed her carrots and an apple. He brushed her in the places he could reach and learned how to avoid being urinated on. He also learned the hard way, horses don't wag their tails.

Other lessons Mark learned quickly were, hens do not voluntarily give up their eggs. Some are downright hateful when one tries to spare them from maternal responsibilities.

The hens with chicks are even more aggressive. They will chase a small boy to the house in a heartbeat if he messes with their newly hatched brood of future picnic fare.

The geese attacked anything that moved. Never mind if harm was intended. Geese are paranoid. They announce loudly that they trust no one.

However, turkeys seem to be unaware of their own existence. Self-preservation is not even high on their priority list.

A visiting varmint, such as a fox, will almost, always find a feast of turkey to be quite satisfactory and leave the other livestock alone. This is a sacrifice the farmer must be willing to make in order to preserve the integrity of his barnyard.

Pigs are a four-legged attitude, Mark learned. If one gets between a pig and his current desire, whether it be food, mud, shade, or another pig, beware!

Goats are the barnyard clowns. They get into all kinds of mischief. They eat anything and everything. Once one ate the plastic handle from the new milk bucket. Another time it ate the rope right off the water well pulley. However, the strangest and most annoying meal he ever had by far, was the seat of Grandpa's tractor!

That goat got a dose of Grandma's bar-be-que sauce for that one.

Mark's favorite animal in the barnyard soon became the old rooster named, Rastus. He was so old, he could no longer crow to announce the arrival of morning. Mark referred to him as the "croupy rooster."

That bird followed Mark around everywhere he went. Mark always kept handfuls of breakfast cereal in his pocket. Every so often he would nudge a few grains of the cereal out of his pocket for the old White Rock to find.

There is something quite sad about a five-year-old boy whose best friend is a geriatric rooster.

That soon changed when Mark began kindergarten. The minister's wife was his teacher and the class was rather small. There were only seventeen students in the pre-k class.

One student was Kevin Joseph Green. Some called him Kay-Jay, others called him Cage for short.

Cage was the class troublemaker. He had no friends and was not interested in making any. His favorite pastime was to torture the little girls and bully the smaller boys. This included just about everyone as Cage was big for his age and his birthday was the same date as the school entry deadline.

All Kindergarteners had to be five years of age by September 1st to be enrolled for that year. Cage's birthday was September 1st. He was several months older than most of his classmates. Several months in a five-year-old's life could make a huge difference in size and attitude.

Kevin Green's dad was the proprietor of a gym, where he trained aspiring boxers and Olympic hopefuls. This may explain why the child was such a bully.

Mark, being a shy and meek individual was no match for Cage. On more than one occasion during the first three weeks of school, Mark came home looking a bit disheveled. No bloody nose or black eye, but his clothing would be ripped, or some of the buttons from his shirt would be missing.

The fact that Mark did not fight back, made Cage more determined to abuse him.

The bullying stopped when Mark showed up at school with his shirttail out, two buttons missing, and his pocket hanging by a few threads.

That day, Mark told Cage he decided to save him the trouble of ripping and rearranging his attire. It worked! Kevin left Mark alone and never bullied him again. They did not become best friends but at least they got along.

Mark's best friend was Billy Jacobs. He was the smallest boy in the class. He wore thick glasses and had about a million freckles.

He was sweet-natured and loved everyone. He especially loved his teacher. He liked to help her with almost any task she needed to be done. His greatest desire was to please his beloved teacher.

When Billy and Mark became inseparable, she acquired another helper. The boys would take turns emptying the wastebasket and picking up crayons, pencils, and paper that were found on the floor.

One day, Mark found a piece of paper on the floor, crumpled into a ball. Just after he'd picked it up, the teacher turned toward him. Assuming he was about to throw it, she reprimanded him. It nearly broke the boy's heart. He could not believe she would even suspect he would do such a thing.

Thinking his teacher didn't like him anymore caused Mark to stop doing his best in school. He would not participate in any of the classroom activities, nor would he join his friend in helping the teacher.

He seemed to have lost all interest in his primary education. He lost the enthusiasm he had for learning to read and sought solitude every chance he got.

Mark used his pet rooster as a listening post. He was often found sitting on the fence rail with that haggard old bird beside him, just unloading his heart out to him. No one else could be as faithful a confidant.

The Host of New Friends

Marcia was making new friends, too. She met Magnolia Powers in her speech class. Magnolia was a dark-skinned African American girl.

The first thing Marcia asked her was if she could call her Maggie. She explained the reason was that her mother was called Maggie and it was short for Margret (which never made sense to Marcia). She thought her mom should have been called Margie.

Having much younger siblings was just one thing the two teens had in common. Maggie had a sister who was nine and a brother who was six and a half. To Maggie's disadvantage, her mother was expecting another baby right at graduation time.

Second families are a common occurrence when a second marriage is in the mix. Maggie was born after her parents separated. Her father's parents played a huge part in the demise of her parent's relationship.

They refused to allow their son to be the head of his own household. They butted into everything. Dictating where they should live, where he should work, what doctor should deliver the baby, everything!

Starting out in marriage was difficult enough without having to take all the criticism and so-called free advice. The marriage dissolved after only sixteen months. But by then Magnolia was already on the way.

Sadly, Magnolia never knew her father, another similarity the two girls shared.

The girls compared notes on how life had been for them and discovered they were kindred souls. Their lifestyles were parallel to one another and their common threads bonded them tightly together.

When Amanda Band found out Magnolia's middle name was Blossom, she teased the girl relentlessly. Later, Marcia discovered Amanda's middle name is Amanda Lynn Band, which turned the tables. After that, no one made fun of anyone else's name. Happily, the teasing was curtailed before they learned Marcia's middle name was Lilly bell.

People can be so cruel to each other. It seemed to be a natural part of growing up to be the butt of someone's joke at least once in a person's life. Often it was ongoing. When they find your tender underbelly, you are doomed. They will look for a way to push your buttons, even if they have to create those buttons for you.

Kids have ridiculed each other for everything from eye color to shoe size, nothing is sacred. Every little thing about a person is a possible target. The more reaction they get, the more targets they look for to throw their painful darts at. God forbid if they should hit a sore spot that causes an open reaction. One may as well draw a bull's eye on himself.

Just as Mark had to toughen up to his bully, Maggie and Marcia had to as well. It took a while, but they managed to let everyone know they were not going to let anyone get under their skin. Soon others who had endured the spikes of Amanda and her cronies joined Marcia and Maggie. Their circle of friends began to grow larger and healthier.

Soon the group of misfits was the elite and formerly popular group who became the outcasts.

Accepting people (warts and all) creates a lot of warty friends. Everyone has an imperfection or two they must deal with.

The Howard Hoedown

Grandma and Grandpa Howard would soon be celebrating their fifty-fifth wedding anniversary. They were married when Grandma was just eighteen years old. However, it would be 23 years after they were married before Maggie would be born. They had all but given up on ever having children. Ruthie came shortly after Maggie. Those two little girls were the delight of their parents' lives.

Grandpa was so shocked upon learning of his wife's first pregnancy, that he could not speak for days. All he could do was grin. He was so sure the baby would be a boy, he would always say, "When my boy gets here…"

When his son turned out to be a daughter, he wasn't the least bit disappointed. He loved her from the word "go." Being joined a short time later by her sister, he couldn't have been happier.

Once again, at age 75, his happiness made him as giddy as any new father could be.

The kids were like a fountain of youth for him, a rejuvenating tonic. All who knew the old man said so. He had found a reason to rejoin the human race. Before his grandchildren came, he was hard to be around. His doom and gloom attitude negatively affected everyone he came in contact with. He seemed to find disapproval in just about everything.

Can you picture a 75-year-old man sitting on the floor putting large puzzle pieces in place and clapping his hands in honest glee with three little tykes beside him?

He especially enjoyed the double hugs he got from the twin girls as one twin on each side snuggled in close for a hug, he reveled in it. Then when Mark joined in to complete a group hug, the old man was in heaven. Mark was his 'compadre.'

Being outnumbered by females in the home compelled the menfolk to bond even more.

Friends and neighbors from the community planned to throw the Howard's a party to celebrate their anniversary. Mrs. Nance was the primary hostess with Mrs. Leonard, Magnolia's mother, and Aunt Ruthie, both who acted as co-hostesses.

Again, the little yard around the Howard home was filled with festivities. Everything from the checkered tablecloths to the hanging lanterns was bright and cheery. The Thornton's provided the beef for the barbeque and all others brought covered dishes. No one left hungry.

The Fiddler's Three supplied the music for the square dance and the cloggers. A good time was had by all.

Having all their friends in one place made the Howard's realize just how fortunate they were to have them. There were over one hundred people, consisting of men, women, and children at that hoedown.

Guests competed in such games as tug-o-war, horseshoes, hat toss, and greased pig chase. Lance III caught the pig. He trapped it behind the trough at the side of the house. The prize was a jar of Grandma's mint jelly and a five-dollar bill.

Later Lance used the five dollars to take Marcia to the picture show.

As the last of the guests left the party, Marcia gathered up all the throwaways. Grandma and Grandpa each carried a sleeping twin, up to their room. Although both needed a bath, Grandma didn't have the heart to wake them or the strength to carry out the task.

Mark had taken himself to bed around 11:00 p.m. What a marvelous day it had been. Friends, family, and fun, a combination that can't be beaten!

The Hunk of Junk

Several years ago, Grandpa took a temporary job with Mr. Mills who was a licensed auctioneer. He had landed a contract to liquidate a huge estate and he hired Grandpa to help catalog the items and transport them to the auction barn.

While taking inventory of the many pieces of Jewelry, Mr. Mills came across a lady's dinner ring. It had a sizable space where a stone had once nestled. It looked like the shank of the ring had been cut from the hand that wore it.

Mr. Mills assumed it had little or no value and offered it to Grandpa. Although he graciously accepted it, he was not at all impressed with the ring. He knew Grandma would never wear it.

After returning home later that evening, Grandpa wrapped the ring in his bandana, put it in a tobacco can and stored the can at the top of his closet. He thought nothing more of it than a hunk of junk and promptly forgot it.

When Marcia began talking about getting married. They all put their heads together to come up with ideas of how they could pay for the wedding. The conversation reminded him of the ring and he made a mental note to have it appraised.

Marcia and Lance III planned a large church wedding. They wanted to be married when they were both twenty years old. By then the twins would be seven and Mark would be almost ten. Most assuredly, they would be members of the wedding party.

Marcia pictured the girls in pink dresses and serving as flower girls. She imagined them walking down the center aisle of the church, tossing pink and red rose petals along the way. She could picture Mark in a tuxedo handing her the ring she would place on her beloved's hand as she vowed to love him for the rest of her life. She thought about the delicate, small, diamond ring he would place on her finger along with the promise to be faithful to her all the days of his life.

The Hand Off

As the wedding day approached, many questions arose. There was no doubt, Marcia and Lance III were very much in love.

One night when Lance and the Nance's came over for supper, the subject of giving the bride away came up. It is traditional that the father of the bride gives her away. However, since Marcia did not know who her father was. It was no question, her grandfather would give her away.

Still, Marcia began thinking about her natural father. She wondered w*ho he was. Did he still live in Ohio? Was he rich? Would he want to be a part of her life now that she had grown up?*

Marcia knew she did not look like her father. The picture on her bedroom wall was proof of that. But did she possess any of his other attributes?

For years, Aunt Ruthie had been keeping a secret. She knew who her sister, Maggie had been intimate with. Many times Ruthie was posted as a lookout when Maggie was entertaining a beau in the barn. She was not entirely aware of what was going on in the barn at the time, but she knew her sister was not willing to get caught at it.

Ruthie saw it only as a way to earn money for candy and such. The boys would always pay her for her post sentry duties.

One of those boys was none other than Lance Allen, Jr.! When Ruthie finally confessed Maggie's antics to Marcia, she was mortified!

The Horrible Secret

Kork Adams was one of the other possibilities. He was now a mechanic at the auto garage owned by Greg Saunders. Greg was also another possibility.

Kork was married to Patsy Williams and they had two boys. Kork was also an alcoholic. He was not the town drunk, but he was a close runner up. Greg gave Kork the job out of pity for his family. Greg never gave Kork his own paycheck. Every Friday, he gave it to Kork's wife. Patsy would in-turn give Kork $10 and by sundown, he would be falling down drunk.

Greg was a conscientious businessman. He owned the garage outright. No bank held him at their mercy. He also owned the diner and the bowling alley. He was married to Lelia Foster. They had no children and never wanted any.

Lelia was vain about her appearance and would not allow a pregnancy to distort her good figure. She was quite the socialite. Hosting dinner parties were a way of life for her. She could be counted on to throw at least one dinner party every season. Each one had to be more lavish than the last. She would begin planning the next party, even before the cake crumbs were vacuumed from the floor of the current one.

Greg and Lelia never came to any of the get-togethers held at the Howard's farm.

The third and final candidate (as far as Ruthie knew) for fatherhood was Jeremy Pringle. He was a high school teacher who never married. Marcia secretly hoped he was her father as she already liked him. She did not hold it against any of the prospective fathers for not owning up to their parentage of her. She was not sure they ever knew she was conceived in that old barn. No one knew as Maggie was only three weeks pregnant when she left.

If Lance Allen, Jr. was her father, that would make her fiancé her half-brother. That issue was more of a concern to Marcia than anything else.

Nothing could stop the tears from falling. Marcia cried for days. The thought of not being able to marry Lance was the worst-case scenario that could be a hindrance to her and Lance's plans.

They just had to go to the big city and get a sibling DNA test done. There was no such thing when Marcia was firstborn.

If Lance, Jr. was her father, Marcia could not marry Lance III. The test must be done. Not to prove who her father was, but more so to prove who he wasn't.

It was not necessary to have Lance, Jr.'s co-operation. The genetic material found in Lance III and Marcia's DNA would have to be a 25% genetic match to determine they were half-siblings.

After the test was administered and they had both suffered through the waiting period until the results came in the mail, to the relief of the young couple, the test revealed no genetic match between Marcia and Lance III. The wedding was on!!!

Nevertheless, in spite of her original feelings regarding who her father was, Marcia discovered she did in fact, want to know more than ever, who her real father was.

She began to wonder how she could get the other three candidates to comply? Could she secretly collect DNA samples from each of them? What would she do when paternity was revealed? Would she confront him? Would she remain silent, or be disappointed? Would she be an heiress? Would she discover she had half brothers and sisters? What a can of worms she would be opening.

The Human Factor

Marcia watched as Greg tossed a toothpick into the wastebasket just before he exited the diner. She waited until he was out of sight and then casually walked over to the wastebasket to retrieve it and carefully placed it in a plastic bag. She walked into the bathroom and entered a stall where she removed a permanent black marker from her purse and used it to print Greg's name across the front of the bag.

The next day, Marcia pulled up to Kork's garage and jumped out of the vehicle.

"Hi, he said. "What can I do for you?"

"Hi, My car cut off on me down the road a piece. I finally, got it to turn over but I was worried, I might not make it back home. Can you take a look at it for me?"

"Sure thing." Kork pops the hood and begins looking around and shaking hoses when he snatched his hand out quickly. "Ouch!"

"Oh, did you hurt yourself?"

"Just a little cut is all."

He reached into his back pocket and pulled out a handkerchief to wipe away the blood from the cut. Afterward, he laid the handkerchief down on the shop table and went into his office to get a Band-Aid from his first aid kit. Marcia seized the opportunity while Kork was in his office, to pick up the handkerchief and quickly stuff it into a zip lock bag and shove it into her purse. She quietly put the hood of the car down, jumped in the car, and peeled out of the garage without so much as a backward look.

While at school she took Mr. Pringle's half-eaten lunch tray to the counter where the dishes and trays were stacked for washing. She cleverly pocketed his napkin after putting it in a Ziplock baggie. "There!" She had all the specimens she needed.

Getting up the nerve to collect all the samples was easy. Getting up the nerve to actually have them tested was extremely stressful. It was like playing a game of Russian Roulette, only with a bullet in all but one chamber.

Marcia thought, if it is Mr. Pringle, I will tell him so. If it is Kork, I'll kill myself, and if it is Greg, well… I'll take that secret to my grave.

The idea of having an alcoholic for a father disturbed Marcia greatly. The possibility of having a well-to-do father was less uncomfortable, but Greg's wife would be impossible to take. In a small town, everybody knew everybody's business. Marcia had already heard Greg's wife was much too controlling and would possibly be a hindrance to her developing a relationship with Greg.

Marcia felt she could be content knowing her father was a school teacher. She also had aspirations of becoming one someday.

The results of the DNA test showed, neither Greg nor Kork was Marcia's father. However, there was a problem with Jeremy Pringle's DNA. Unfortunately, it was not enough DNA material on the napkin to prove positively that

Jeremy Pringle was her father. Nevertheless, it was enough for Marcia!

The following day at school, Marcia bolstered her courage enough to ask Mr. Pringle if she could talk to him after school.

The hands on the clock appeared to be standing still. It seemed like three o'clock would never come. All day long Marcia went over and over in her mind what she would say to Mr. Pringle. She thought about how she would bring up the subject and how she would prepare herself for his reaction.

Finally, the bell rang! Her heart picked up speed. Her temples were throbbing. When everyone had cleared the room, Marcia shut the door. She sat back down at her desk in the front of the classroom.

Clearing her throat, Marcia's voice still cracked as she spoke. "Mr. Pringle, do you remember my mother? Her name was Margret Howard. You dated her when you were about sixteen."

"Yes, of course I do. She was my first love. We wanted to get married, but we were too young."

"Are you saying, you were in love with her?"

"Yes, and I guess I still am."

"I never married because I never found anyone I cared about as much or more than I cared about Maggie." He lowered his head as he spoke.

Marcia, cleared her throat again, "Well, I think you may be my father." Marcia searched his face for a hint of denial in his eyes. However, to her surprise, she found only tears.

"I did not know she was pregnant, she never told me. I never heard a word from her or anything about her until you and your sisters and brother arrived. I thought you were Mr. Murphy's daughter."

Marcia looked at him and said, At least now I know I was conceived in love. Did my mother love you?"

"I believe she did," Mr. Pringle said with a smile of remembrance on his face. "I know I was not the only boy she was ever with. But I know I was the only one who loved her. I begged her to go steady with me and leave the other boys alone, but she just wouldn't. I told her we could get married if she wanted to. She said she would marry me if I would take her away from here. I couldn't leave, so she left without me."

Marcia listened quietly as her father told her how Maggie and he had made love only once. They planned to elope as soon as Jeremy had his seventeenth birthday.

Three weeks later, she was gone.

The Hellbender

It was obvious that Lance Allen, Jr. was on a path of self-destruction his entire life. It started when he was in third grade. He picked a fight with the biggest kid in school. He lost the fight and three of his teeth. Luckily, they were not his permanent teeth or he would have been the only nine year old with dentures.

At the age of 12, he stole a bicycle right out of the showroom of the Western Auto store. His daddy bailed him out of that one by leaning on the manager. He threatened to foreclose on his mortgage if he insisted on pressing charges on his precious little boy.

When Lance, Jr. was 14, he decided it was time he drove the family car. He ended up in the hospital instead of juvie when he attempted to impress his friends by trying to outrun a train. He lost that fight, too. He suffered two broken ribs, a gash in his knee that cost him eleven stitches, and he bit a hole in his tongue.

There were other incidents that caused Jr. to narrowly escape jail, the hospital, or the funeral parlor. He was always in some kind of trouble.

Trouble with the law was the one thing he looked to his father to remedy each time he committed a misdemeanor.

Lance, Jr. was an embarrassment to his mother as well as his father. She all but dropped out of the social scene when Lance, Jr. started to openly misbehave.

Lance started to drink heavily when he reached his twenties. His drinking buddy was none other than, Kork.

Kork's wife was expecting their third child. She was in her fourth month of pregnancy when Kork came home one Friday evening drunk and spoiling for a fight. The kids were already in bed but he made his wife get them up. When she protested, he slapped her across the face. She fell against the dining room table and onto the floor.

Kork was too drunk to drive her to the hospital. She lay on the kitchen floor for five hours. There was no phone in the house so that she could call for help. She miscarried a baby girl that day.

Kork spent the next week at the garage. He was too ashamed to go home and face his wife. He knew how much she'd wanted a baby girl, and so did he.

Lance, Jr. never married. He had been engaged once but the girl found out what a cad he was and broke off the engagement. At first, she was reluctant to believe any of the tales she'd heard about him. She thought the tale-tellers were just jealous of her good fortune to have found a man of his financial worth.

The opinion of the entire community was, for a man of worth, he was quite worthless. That assessment was often the same point of view held by his parents.

If, he would just for once in his life, do something to make his father proud, his destructive social behavior would have been more tolerable.

It should not have been that difficult to please a man with Lance Allen, Sr.'s values. The thing that rubbed him the wrong way with his son was, Lance, Jr. never came out on top. There was never any profit in his ventures. Most often, it cost his father a great deal as well. The lawyer fees alone for the rape trial were over $122,000.

Of course, that didn't even put a dent in Lance Allen, Sr.'s pocket. It was the idea that his son was a constant liability, rather than an asset that bothered him the most. He'd hoped that his son would be a winner in life, just as Lance, Sr. had considered himself to be. Instead, he's shown at every turn, he was a loser.

The Heartbreak

The day had finally come that they'd both been waiting for. Lance Allen III and Marcia Lilly bell Howard would say their "I do's."

Thanks to Grandpa's ring, the wedding would go exactly as planned. The money from the sale of that ring was instrumental in paying for the most beautiful ceremony a bride could hope for. It also put a sizable nest egg in the bank for their future. Now Marcia would be able to go to college and get her degree so she could become a teacher.

However, the morning of the wedding, Grandpa woke up feeling exhausted, he was more tired than he had been after sleeping all night. His breathing was labored and his body hurt all over. Grandma refused to allow him to get out of bed. If he did not improve before the wedding was set to begin, he would not be able to walk Marcia down the aisle. The mere thought of that possibility broke his heart.

There was a gentleman who was willing to be his stand-in should he not be well enough to do the honors.

Jeremy Pringle was more than happy to give his daughter away. Though he had only found her a few months ago. He had developed a very good relationship with Marcia, her fiancé, and the whole family for that matter.

Grandpa, couldn't make it. He was too weak and the doctor told him to rest and avoid stress. What could be more stressful than getting a man who had worn overalls for fifty years into a tuxedo?

Marcia's father walked her down the aisle. When asked, "Who gives this bride away?" Jeremy Pringle replied, "Her grandparents and I do."

This was the next best thing to having her grandfather there.

Grandpa Howard remained confined to his bed for a month after the wedding.

The Honeymoon

The honeymoon had to be cut short so Marcia could help Grandma tend to the children.

They had planned to go to Niagara Falls but they felt it was best to be home to look after things. They agreed to take the honeymoon at another time. They understood the honeymoon was a state of mind and not a place in time.

Grandpa gradually got better, but he'd slowed down considerably. He was not able to keep up with the children as much as he used to when they first arrived.

An active 12-year-old and two seven year old's had become too difficult for him to manage.

Over time, the children had grown to be independent. All three children could ride the horse. They all could tend to the barn chores and Mark could even drive the big red tractor.

Mandy learned to cook and liked doing so. Melissa liked to sew and keep the house clean. Soon they would be looking after the Grandparents.

Marcia went to college and Lance got a job selling new cars at the local Ford dealership. They all lived together in that great big farmhouse as one big happy family.

Everyone was ecstatic when Marcia asked Grandma to unlock the nursery.

Marcia and Lance had been married for six months when she became pregnant.

When the baby was born, he was named Howard Murphy Allen. They asked Jeremy if it would be alright if they called him Jerry, after him.

Howard Murphy as not a particularly nice-sounding name but it honored the two men who had been most important in Marcia's life. She had to fit Jeremy in somehow because he had become important to her as well.

She was not about to name her baby, Pringle. She thought back to her old school friend, Amanda Band.

Grandma and Grandpa signed the farm over to Lance and Marcia in the event they could no longer care for themselves, the State would not take the farm in place of payment to the County for nursing home care.

That situation never materialized. They both died at home. Grandpa died of a sudden heart attack at the age of 80 and Grandma died peacefully in her sleep at the age of 79.

Marcia got legal custody of her brother and twin sisters she'd helped to raise from infancy.

She and Lance had four boys of their own.

The Allen farm was known far and wide as the happiest home in Ohio.

The Hero

Lance Allen, Jr. was involved in a car wreck that nearly took his life. It was seven hours before the overturned car was even discovered on a road that was rarely traveled. He was pinned under the vehicle for over 13 hours, while rescuers tried relentlessly to extract him from the gnarled mass of machinery.

By the time he was finally freed from the mangled vehicle, He was in critical condition. A rod had pierced his kidney and he'd lost a lot of blood. He also had multiple fractures and contusions.

When Lance III found out about the accident, he was beside himself. He rushed to the hospital to see if he was a match for a kidney transplant for his father.

He meant to say, a blood transfusion, but he said kidney transplant, so that is what they tested him for. He was a perfect match for a kidney, right down to the size.

Although the man had caused everyone he loved great sorrow, Lance III could not resist helping his father. He did ungrudgingly donate one of his kidneys to his father.

By the time Lance, Jr. went home, he had no desire to find trouble. He had a higher regard for others and he felt remorse for the first time in his life.

Many follow up appointments back and forth to the hospital, made a new man of Lance Allen, Jr. It was during this turning point, he desired to be a part of the life of a son, whom he'd once denied was his own. The son who sacrificed his kidney for a man he felt was worthy of it.

Lance, Jr. also wanted to be a part of his grandchildren's lives.

He apologized to his son, for having defiled his mother so many years ago.

Most of all, he begged Lance to forgive him for not being the father he should have been.

Home In the Heartland

Lance Allen, Jr. made it clear to his father he wanted his son to be included in the family enterprises and wealth that were amassed overtime. The wealth he so foolishly had taken for granted.

All Lance and Marcia wanted was security for their children.

Lance, Jr. drew up a trust fund that at full maturity would be worth 410,000 for each child. Each child would receive his or her share of the money on their twenty-first birthday.

Also, they would each receive $30,000 a year plus ten thousand for each child and twenty thousand for their wives, should they marry.

Life sure has a funny way of correcting mistakes, doesn't it?

//The End//

Biography

Renna Jo was born, Renna Jo Herriott in Fort Worth, TX in 1948. She attended Polytechnic High School. She graduated in 1966. She married her childhood playmate the following year.

As young adults, she and her husband were house parents and foster parents to many troubled youths. Many of them did not know who their parents were.

This spawned the storyline for Home In the Heartland.